Fact Finders®

It's Back to School ... Way Back!

School in COLONIAL AMERICA

by Shelley Swanson Sateren

CAPSTONE PRESS
a capstone imprint

Fact Finder Books are published by Capstone Press,
1710 Roe Crest Drive, North Mankato, Minnesota 56003.
www.mycapstone.com

Library of Congress Cataloging-in-Publication Data
Names: Sateren, Shelley Swanson, author.
Title: School in colonial America / by Shelley Swanson Sateren.
Description: North Mankato, Minnesota: Capstone Press, [2017] |
Series: Fact finders. Going back to school ... way back! | Includes bibliographical references and index.
Identifiers: LCCN 2015048719 | ISBN 9781515720973 (library binding) |
ISBN 9781515721017 (paperback) | ISBN 9781515721055 (ebook pdf)
Subjects: LCSH: Education—United States—History—17th century—Juvenile literature. |
Education—United States—History—18th century—Juvenile literature. |
Schools—United States—History—17th century—Juvenile literature. |
Schools—United States—History—18th century—Juvenile literature. |
United States—History—Colonial period, ca. 1600-1775—Juvenile literature.
Classification: LCC LA206 .S28 2017 | DDC 370.973—dc23
LC record available at https://lccn.loc.gov/2015048719

Editorial Credits
Editor: Nikki Potts
Designer: Kayla Rossow
Media Researcher: Jo Miller
Production Specialist: Kathy McColley

Photo Credits
Alamy: Pat & Chuck Blackley, 19; Corbis: Bettmann, cover; Getty Images: Bettmann, 23; Granger, NYC - All rights reserved, 10, 21, 24, 27; North Wind Picture Archives, 5, 6, 7, 8, 13, 15, 17, 28; Shutterstock: Africa Studio, cover (background), Black Hill Design (berries), 29, lendy16, 29 (feathers), tomertu, 22; Design Elements: Shutterstock: Frank Rohde, iulias, marekuliasz, Undrey

Printed and bound in the USA.
009671F16

TABLE OF CONTENTS

Chapter 1

LIVING IN THE AMERICAN COLONIES

Europeans began building colonies along the eastern coast of North America in the 1600s. Some colonists came to freely practice their religion. Other settlers came to claim a piece of land and start a new life. Some came as **indentured servants**. Wealthy colonists paid their passage. In return servants agreed to work for them for four to seven years.

American Indians had lived in North America for thousands of years. At first some welcomed the newcomers and helped them survive in unfamiliar surroundings. Later many colonists fought the American Indians and forced them off their land.

By the mid-1700s, 13 British colonies had formed along the eastern coast of North America. The colonies were divided into three separate regions—the New England colonies, the middle colonies, and the southern colonies.

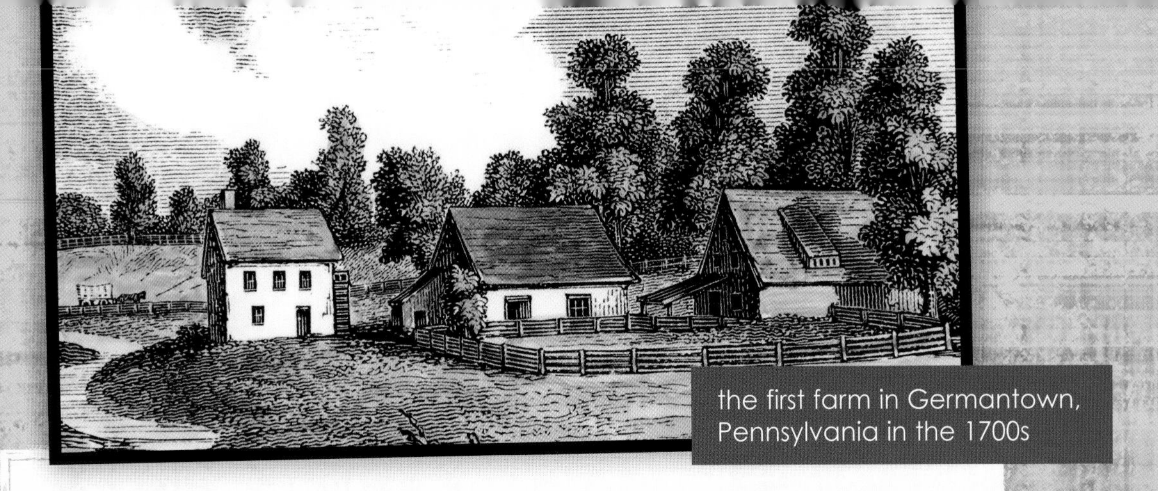

the first farm in Germantown, Pennsylvania in the 1700s

The New England colonies were densely populated. Many colonists lived near towns and cities. Most were farmers, shop owners, or tradespeople.

Farmers who lived in the middle colonies grew large fields of grain. They supplied the British colonies with grain for breads. This area was known as the "breadbasket."

In the southern colonies most people lived in rural areas. Most southern colonists owned small farms. But some colonists lived on large plantations. These plantations were mostly self-sufficient communities. Plantations depended on enslaved Africans to farm fields of tobacco, rice, and **indigo**.

indentured servant—a type of slave who works for someone else for a period of time in return for payment of travel and living costs

indigo—plant that produces a deep-blue dye

Great Britain ruled the 13 American colonies. British officials began putting taxes on many goods brought into the colonies. The British government set the taxes. The colonists felt the taxes were unfair, and they began to talk about forming their own country.

King George III did not want to give up the American colonies. He sent soldiers to enforce English laws. Colonists formed their own army to fight the English soldiers. This action led to the beginning of the Revolutionary War (1775–1783).

With many fathers away at war, families had extra work at home. Family members worked together to plant and harvest crops. Children helped with extra chores.

Many children did not attend school during the Revolutionary War. Women sometimes taught students while schoolmasters were away at battle.

Colonists protest the Stamp Act in New York City, 1765.

In 1781 the British Army surrendered. The colonists officially gained their independence two years later. Leaders from the 13 colonies named their new country the United States of America.

Minutemen were important fighters during the Revolutionary War. They were volunteer soldiers who were trained to be ready to fight 'at a moment's notice.'

Chapter 2

SCHOOLING IN THE COLONIES

In the 1600s, most colonial parents wanted their children to receive a basic education. They wanted their children to learn to read and to study the Bible. But few schools existed in North America. Many families lived in **rural** areas, far from towns and schools. They did not have transportation to send their children to school. Many children learned to read and write at home.

A grandmother teaches a child to read.

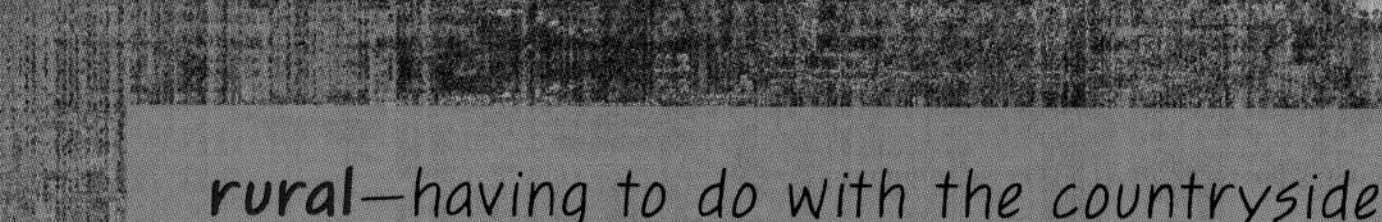

rural—*having to do with the countryside*

MAP OF COLONIAL SCHOOLS

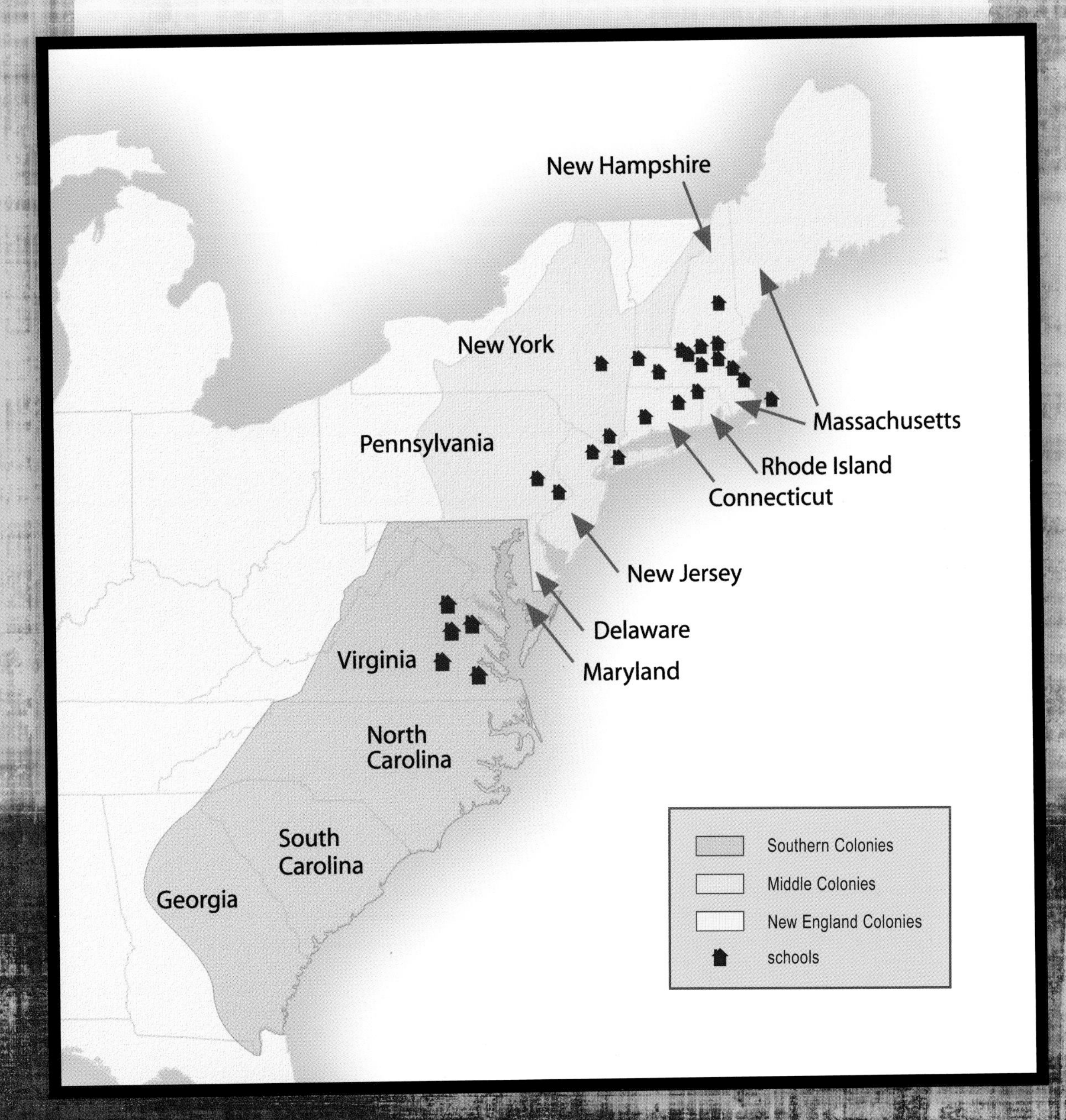

Pilgrim children on their way to school in 1700

Missionaries

Missionaries set up many of the first schools in the colonies. They wanted to teach people about Christianity. In the mid-1600s, New England colonists built several American Indian schools. Missionaries worked at these schools teaching American Indians how to read and study the Bible. African slaves were not allowed to go to school. But some former slaves were set free. Missionaries ran schools for free African-Americans.

missionary—person who works on behalf of a religious group to spread the group's faith

FACT Schools called academies were established in the colonies during the mid-1700s. These schools offered a variety of classes from history and philosophy to navigation and sewing.

Colonists built more schools as towns grew larger. Most schools opened in thickly populated New England towns. The General Court of Massachusetts passed a new school law in 1647. Townships of at least 50 families were required to hire a teacher. Because townspeople lived close together, most children walked to school. Many children who lived on nearby farms walked 3 to 4 miles to get to the village schoolhouse.

Town governments expected parents to teach their children basic subjects. Many towns built grammar schools where children who already had these basic skills could begin preparing for college. Grammar schools offered classes in geography, spelling, reading, English grammar, and Latin.

By the late 1600s the New England colonies had more schools than any other region in America. New England became known for the high quality of its schools. New Englanders were very religious. They wanted all children to be able to read and study the Bible. Most New England schools taught the three Rs—reading, writing, and arithmetic.

Few schools existed in the middle colonies. A religious group called the Quakers settled in the region. Quakers believed in a practical education. William Penn founded the Friends Public School in Philadelphia in 1689. Penn wanted all children to be taught a useful trade or skill. Quakers opened many private schools.

FACT

After the Revolutionary War, New Englanders set up city, or district, schools run by town governments. Many district schools did not receive enough money to stay open for more than a few months at a time.

Young boys apprenticed to craftsmen, such as woodworkers, who taught them useful skills and how to use tools.

Many children from the New England and middle colonies became **apprentices**. They apprenticed with tradesmen for several years to learn crafts such as blacksmithing, carpentry, painting, shipbuilding, and sailmaking. Girls received apprenticeships in needlework, sewing, and other crafts.

apprentice—*a person who works for and learns from a skilled professional for a set amount of time*

In the southern colonies, farms and plantations were spread far apart. Most parents instructed their children at home in the evenings.

For some rural children, one-room schools called field schools offered a basic education. These schoolhouses stood on unused farmland. Traveling schoolmasters sometimes taught in these rural schoolhouses.

Some wealthy plantation owners sent their children to England for an education. Others hired tutors to teach their children.

Colonial Schoolmasters

In colonial times most schoolmasters were men. Sometimes women held "dame schools" for young children. Children gathered in the woman's home and learned basic reading and writing skills. Classes were sometimes held for older girls to teach them reading, arithmetic, manners, Latin, and French.

Some southern children took lessons from local pastors who traveled from house to house. Colonial schoolmasters did not make much money. Teachers sometimes stayed with families. In this way they received **room and board** instead of a salary.

room and board—lodging and food, forming part of someone's salary

Colonial women taught girls the responsibilities of running a household. Girls needed to know how to cook, sew, garden, and finish daily chores. Most girls did not receive an education beyond basic reading and writing. In the late 1700s, some colonial parents sent their daughters to private finishing schools. The teachers taught needlework, music, art, and manners.

A young girl learns to sew.

Chapter 3

THE NEW ENGLAND COLONIAL SCHOOLHOUSE

Most New England schoolhouses in colonial times were one-room, clapboard buildings. Colonists filled gaps between boards with a clay and grass mixture called chinking. Five or six small windows lined the side walls to provide light for the students. Some schoolhouses were painted red or yellow.

Schoolhouses often had a large fireplace at one end of the room. Some parents helped pay for their children's education by supplying firewood for the schoolhouse. If parents forgot to send firewood to school, their children were made to sit in the seat farthest from the fireplace.

Colonial schoolhouses had a raised platform near the fireplace for the schoolmaster's desk. Sloping shelves lined the side walls and served as writing platforms. Children faced the platforms, sitting on long, backless wooden benches. Some schoolhouses had double desks. Two children sat at each desk.

an early colonial schoolroom in New England

Chapter 4

THE MIDDLE COLONY AND SOUTHERN COLONY SCHOOLHOUSES

Some of the first schoolhouses in the middle colonies were log structures. The schools sometimes had floors made of split, smoothed logs. Colonists stuck sticks into the walls and placed boards on top to use as desktops.

In the southern colonies schools often were abandoned livestock barns or sheds. Even plantation owners' children attended schools in crude, unfurnished structures.

Most colonial schoolhouses had a schoolyard. During the day children went outside for a short recess. They played marbles, tag, or hoops.

Whipping Posts and Whispering Sticks

Schoolmasters were very strict during the 1600s and 1700s. They expected students to perform their **recitations** well, pay attention during lessons, and behave in a respectful manner. Schoolmasters punished students for disruptions and mistakes.

Many schools had a whipping post outside the building. Schoolmasters tied misbehaving children to the post and hit them with a leather strap called a rattan.

In the classroom teachers often quieted children with whispering sticks. Schoolmasters made students who were caught whispering hold the wooden sticks in their mouths. Whispering sticks sometimes had strings attached to tie the sticks to the children's heads. Other schoolmasters pinched students' noses with slit sticks. Students kept the sticks on their noses until the schoolmaster took them off.

Some New England schoolmasters made children wear a dunce cap if they did not learn their lessons. Students had to wear tall, cone-shaped hats and sit on stools separated from the rest of the class.

replica of the first school in Harrodsburg, Kentucky

recitation—*the action of repeating something aloud from memory*

Chapter 5

A COLONIAL SCHOOL DAY

Schoolmasters separated colonial students into several classes. They grouped children according to the level of their skills. Boys and girls sometimes attended separate schools.

The school day often began with a Bible reading. Students took turns reading that day's passages. Each student stood while reading.

Books were rare and expensive. Students were careful with their books. They often used thumb papers to protect the pages. Students folded small pieces of newspaper or wrapping paper around the pages where their thumbs held the book. Students also used tweezerlike tools called page turners to help protect the pages.

Many colonial children studied from the New England Primer. The early Primer was a book of short **devotions**, the **Lord's Prayer**, the Ten Commandments, and a few **psalms**. The book covers were made from thin pieces of oak, covered with a coarse brown or blue paper.

Young children studied from hornbooks. The wooden study boards were shaped like paddles. Hornbooks had a piece of paper attached to the paddle. On it was printed the ABCs, the Lord's Prayer, a reading lesson, and a few simple sentences. The paper was covered with a thin, clear sheet called horn. The covering protected the paper.

Many young students also studied with battledores. These illustrated primers had two or three pages with content similar to a hornbook. A folded flap secured the pages in place.

18th century American colonial hornbook

devotion—a prayer, worship, or other religious activity

Lord's Prayer—a prayer said by Christians; this prayer appears in the Bible

psalm—religious song or poem

Some students owned revolving alphabets made from two small wooden disks. A piece of paper was between the disks. One side of the paper had the alphabet. The other side had a series of syllables. A small opening was cut near the outer edge of each disk. The paper revolved between the disks, revealing letters and syllables in the openings.

Penmanship was an important subject in colonial schools. The schoolmaster made quill pens by cutting the ends off goose quills at an angle. Children dipped the pointed end of the quill into the inkpot. After writing several letters students needed to dip the pen again. But ink often froze in the inkpots during the winter. Students thawed the ink and thinned it with water.

penmanship—*the art of writing by hand*

Colonial schoolteachers had to be good pen makers and pen menders. The shaping of feathers into pens required fine skills. It often took a teacher two hours each day to make and mend enough pens for the whole class.

Schoolmasters seldom gave students paper to use because it was so expensive. School paper was rough, dark, and sometimes unruled. Children often wrote on strips of birch bark instead.

A schoolmaster sharpens his quill.

Students often learned to write from copybooks. The books encouraged kind and respectful behavior. By copying the sentences children improved their handwriting and learned how to behave well.

In the afternoon students gave their recitations. Students recited homework lessons from their readers every day.

a 1790s New England grammar school

Many grammar schools also taught students arithmetic. Most colonial children did not own their own printed arithmetic books. Early arithmetic books, such as *The Schoolmaster's Assistant*, were printed for schoolmasters to consult.

Some New England schools taught history, geography, and Latin. Many history books were religious. In 1708 *The History of Genesis* was published. It was named after the first book of the Bible. Other books also existed for school-age children. One was *The Child's Weeks-work*. This textbook contained daily lessons for four weeks. It included proverbs and fables. It taught children lessons on **morals** and behavior. In addition to these lessons, *The Child's Weeks-work* had a prayer section and a **catechism**, which children used to learn the teachings of the Bible.

morals—beliefs about what is right and wrong

catechism—a collection of questions and answers that are used to teach people about the Christian religion

Chapter 6

EXHIBITION DAY

The most exciting day for children was exhibition day. Schoolmasters held the event at the end of the term. Students showed parents and townspeople what they had learned during the school year.

Students displayed their penmanship by writing an exhibition piece. They wrote short essays on happiness, friendship, obedience, and kindness. Children often recited short essays or Bible passages.

Schoolmasters also held public "spells" on exhibition day. During a spell children lined up and schoolmasters gave them words to spell out loud. The schoolmaster often selected words from *The London Spelling Book* or Webster's *The American Spelling Book*. Students who misspelled their words took their seats. The student left standing at the end was the winner.

Noah Webster's Spelling Book

In colonial times people did not have set rules for spelling. Many colonists spelled the same word in various ways. They often spelled words the way they sounded. For example, colonists might spell "young" as *yong* or *yonge*. They sometimes spelled "himself" as *him self* or *himself*. In the late 1700s, Noah Webster wrote a spelling book to create a simple and uniform system of spelling.

Webster eventually named his book *The American Spelling Book*. Webster continued to expand and improve it. Many people referred to Webster's spelling book as "The Old Blue-back." After the Revolutionary War, Webster's blue-back speller became the main textbook for many students. Eventually these books became the dictionaries many people use today.

86 AN EASY STANDARD

TABLE XXVII.

In all words ending in *ow* unaccented, *w* is ſilent, and *o* has its firſt ſound. Many of theſe words are corrupted in vulgar pronunciation; *follow* is called *foller*, &c. for which reaſon the words of this claſs are collected in the following table.

2 BAr row	bel lows	hal low	win now
bel low	har row	ſhad ow	yel low
bil low	cal low	ſhal low	5 bor row
el bow	mal lows	ſpar row	fol low
fel low	mar row	tal low	mor row
fal low	mead ow	whit low	ſor row
far row	mel low	wid ow	wal low
fur row	min now	wil low	ſwal low
gal lows	nar row	win dow	

TABLE XXVIII.

In the following words, *s* ſounds like *zh*. Thus, *confuſion* is pronounced *confu-zhun*, *bra-ſier*, *bra-zhur*, *o-zier*, *o-zhur*, *viſ ſion*, *vizh-un*, *plea ſure*, *pleazh-ur*.

Note. In this and the following table, the figures ſhew the accented ſyllables, without any other direction.

1 BRA sier	1 am bro sial	de lu sion
cro sier	ad he sion	dif fu sion
gla zier	al lu sion	ef fu sion
o zier	co he sion	ex clu sion
ra ſure	col lu sion	ex plo sion
ho sier	con clu sion	e va sion
ſei zure	con fu sion	a bra sion
fu sion	con tu sion	cor ro sion
		de tru sion

OF PRONUNCIATION. 87

dif plo sion	2 vis ion	di vis ion
em bra ſure	meaſ ure	de cis ion
en clo ſure	pleaſ ure	de ris ion
e ra sion	treaſ ure	e lis ion
il lu sion	leiſ ure	e lys ian
in tru sion	az ure	pre cis ion
in fu sion	2 ab ſciſ ion	pro vis ion
pro fu sion	col lis ion	al lis ion
oc ca sion	con cis ion	re ſciſ ion
ob tru sion		9 2 cir cum cis ion

The compounds and derivatives follow the ſame rule.

FABLE II. *The Country Maid and her Milk pail.*

WHEN men ſuffer their imagination to amuſe them with the proſpect of diſtant and uncertain improvements of their condition; they frequently ſuſtain real loſſes, by their inattention to thoſe affairs in which they are immediately concerned.

spread from the 1795 edition of Noah Webster's *The American Spelling Book*

Colonial students had special days off from school. In the New England colonies schoolchildren had a day off to watch people be publicly punished. Accused criminals were often placed in stocks. The wooden devices locked the criminals' hands or feet. They stayed in stocks for a set number of hours, depending on the crime. Colonists hoped public punishments would stop other colonists from committing similar crimes.

A Puritan man sits in the stocks in Massachusetts Bay Colony in the 1600s.

MAKE A QUILL PEN AND BERRY INK

What You Need for the Berry Ink

- medium bowl
- liquid measuring cup
- ½ cup frozen raspberries or blueberries, thawed
- potato masher
- strainer
- small bowl
- ½ teaspoon salt
- ½ teaspoon vinegar
- ⅛ cup water
- small mixing spoon
- small glass jar with lid, such as a baby food jar
- measuring spoons

What You Need for the Quill Pen

- 1 long bird feather (you can find feathers at most craft stores and hobby shops)
- sharp knife or scissors

What You Do to Make the Berry Ink

1. In the medium-sized bowl mash the berries with the potato masher.
2. Set the strainer over the small bowl. Pour the berry liquid through the strainer. The juice will drip into the small bowl and the strainer will hold the berry pulp.
3. Add salt, vinegar, and water to the berry juice. Stir.
4. Over a sink slowly pour the juice mixture into the jar.
5. Dip a homemade quill pen into your ink to write on paper.
6. Tightly seal the jar with the lid when finished.

What You Do to Make the Quill Pen

1. With an adult's help, cut the quill at a slant using the knife or scissors. The quill is hollow. This hollow area holds the ink.
2. Dip the pointed tip into your ink.
3. After writing with the pen for a while, the point will become dull. Mend the pen by trimming the end with the scissors.

GLOSSARY

apprentice (uh-PREN-tiss)—a person who works for and learns from a skilled professional for a set amount of time

catechism (KAT-uh-ki-zem)—a collection of questions and answers that are used to teach people about the Christian religion

devotion (di-VOH-shuhn)—a prayer, worship, or other religious activity

indentured servant (in-DEN-churd SERV-uhnt)—a type of slave who works for someone else for a period of time in return for payment of travel and living costs

indigo (IN-di-goh)—plant that produces a deep-blue dye

Lord's Prayer (LORDZ PRAY-ur)—a prayer said by Christians; this prayer appears in the Bible

missionary (MISH-uh-ner-ee)—person who works on behalf of a religious group to spread the group's faith

morals (MOR-uhls)—beliefs about what is right and wrong

penmanship (PEN-muhn-ship)—the art of writing by hand

psalm (SAHLM)—religious song or poem

recitation (res-i-TAY-shuhn)—the action of repeating something aloud from memory

rural (RUR-uhl)—having to do with the countryside

room and board (ROOM and BORD)—lodging and food, forming part of someone's salary

READ MORE

Hinman, Bonnie. *The Scoop on School and Work in Colonial America.* Life in the American Colonies. North Mankato, Minn.: Capstone Press, 2012.

Micklos, John Jr. *The Making of the United States from Thirteen Colonies—Through Primary Sources.* The American Revolution Through Primary Sources. Berkeley Heights, N.J.: Enslow Publishers, 2013.

Pratt, Mary. *A Timeline History of the Thirteen Colonies.* Time Trackers: America's Beginnings. Minneapolis: Lerner Publications, 2014.

INTERNET SITES

FactHound offers a safe, fun way to find Internet sites related to this book. All of the sites on FactHound have been researched by our staff.

Here's all you do:

Visit *www.facthound.com*

Type in this code: 9781515720973

CRITICAL THINKING USING THE COMMON CORE

1. What materials were used to build the first schoolhouses in the Middle Colonies? (Key Ideas and Details)
2. Colonists often provided room and board for schoolteachers. What does room and board mean? (Craft and Structure)
3. Take a look at the map on page 9. Which of the three colonial areas had the most schools? (Integration of Knowledge and Ideas)

INDEX